Books by Sigmund Brouwer

Lightning on Ice Series
#1 Rebel Glory
#2 All-Star Pride
#3 Thunderbird Spirit
#4 Winter Hawk Star
#5 Blazer Drive
#6 Chief Honor

Short Cuts Series
#1 Snowboarding to the Extreme . . . Rippin'
#2 Mountain Biking to the Extreme . . . Cliff Dive
#3 Skydiving to the Extreme . . . 'Chute Roll
#4 Scuba Diving to the Extreme . . . Off the Wall

CyberQuest Series
#1 Pharaoh's Tomb
#2 Knight's Honor
#3 Pirate's Cross (available 8/97)
#4 Outlaw Gold (available 10/97)

The Accidental Detectives Mystery Series

Winds of Light Medieval Adventures

Adult Books
Double Helix
Blood Ties

QUEST 2
KNIGHT'S HONOR

SIGMUND BROUWER

Thomas Nelson, Inc.
Nashville

Knight's Honor
Quest 2 in the *CyberQuest* Series

Published in Nashville, Tennessee,
by Tommy Nelson™, a division of Thomas Nelson, Inc.

Managing Editor: Laura Minchew
Project Editor: Beverly Phillips
Cover illustration: Kevin Burke

Library of Congress Cataloging-in-Publication Data

Brouwer, Sigmund, 1959–
   Knight's honor / Sigmund Brouwer.
      p. cm. — (CyberQuest ; #2)
   Summary: As the test of his faith in virtual reality continues,
Mok, a Welfaro from the twenty-first century, finds himself in the
Middle Ages in a castle besieged during the Crusades.
   ISBN 0-8499-4035-4
   [1. Science fiction. 2. Virtual reality—Fiction.
3. Christian life—Fiction.]   I. Title. II. Series: Brouwer,
Sigmund, 1959–   CyberQuest ; #2.
PZ7.B79984Kn 1997
[Fic]—dc21   97-9994
                                                                        CIP
                                                                        AC

Printed in the United States of America
97 98 99 00 01 02 OPM 9 8 7 6 5 4 3 2 1

**To the *Breakaway* readers
who added a lot of fun to the series**

CYBERQUEST SERIES TERMS

BODYWRAP — a sheet of cloth that serves as clothing.

THE COMMITTEE — a group of people dedicated to making the world a better place.

MAINSIDE — any part of North America other than Old Newyork.

MINI-VIDCAM — a hidden video camera.

NETPHONE — a public telephone with a computer keypad. For a minimum charge, users can send e-mail through the Internet.

OLD NEWYORK — the bombed out island of Manhattan transformed into a colony for convicts and the poorest of the poor.

TECHNOCRAT — an upper class person who can read, operate computers, and make much more money than a Welfaro.

'TRIC SHOOTER — an electric gun that fires enough voltage to stun its target.

VIDTRANS — video transmitters.

VIDWATCH — a watch with a mini television screen.

WATERMAN — a person who sells pure water.

WELFARO — a person living in the slums in Old Newyork.

THE GREAT WATER WARS—A.D. 2031. *In the year A.D. 2031 came the great Water Wars. The world's population had tripled during the previous thirty years. Worldwide demand for fresh, unpolluted water grew so strong that countries fought for control of water supplies. The war was longer and worse than any of the previous world wars. When it ended, there was a new world government, called the World United. The government was set up to distribute water among the world countries and to prevent any future wars. But it took its control too far.*

World United began to see itself as all important. After all, it had complete control of the world's limited water supplies. It began to make choices about who was "worthy" to receive water.

Very few people dared to object when World United denied water to criminals, the poor, and others it saw as undesirable. People were afraid of losing their own water if they spoke up.

One group, however, saw that the government's actions were wrong. These people dared to speak—Christians.

They knew that only God should have control

of their lives. They knew that they needed to stand up to the government for those who could not. Because of this, the government began to persecute the Christians and outlawed the Christian church. Some people gave up their beliefs to continue to receive an allotment of government water. Others refused and either joined underground churches or became hunted rebels, getting their water on the black market.

In North America, only one place was safe for the rebel Christians. The island of Old Newyork. The bombings of the great Water Wars had destroyed much of it, and the government used the entire island as a prison. The government did not care who else fled to the slums of those ancient street canyons.

Old Newyork grew in population. While most newcomers were criminals, some were these rebel Christians. Desperate for freedom, they entered this lion's den of lawlessness.

Limited water and supplies were sent from Mainside to Old Newyork, but some on Mainside said that any was too much to waste on the slums. When the issue came up at a World Senate meeting in 2049, it was decided that Old Newyork must be treated like a small country. It would have to provide something to the world in return for water and food.

When this new law went into effect, two things happened in the economy of this giant slum. First, work gangs began stripping steel *from the skyscrapers. Anti-pollution laws on Mainside made it expensive to manufacture new steel. Old steel, then, was traded for food and water.*

Second, when a certain Mainside business genius got caught evading taxes in 2053, he was sent to Old Newyork. There he quickly saw a new business opportunity—slave labor.

Old Newyork was run by criminals and had no laws. Who was there to stop him from forcing people to work for him?

Within a couple of years, the giant slum was filled with bosses who made men, women, and children work at almost no pay. They produced clothing on giant sewing machines and assembled cheap computer products. Even boys and girls as young as ten years old worked up to twelve hours a day.

Christians in Old Newyork, of course, fought against this. But it was a battle the Christians lost over the years. Criminals and factory bosses used ruthless violence to control the slums.

Christianity was forced to become an underground movement in the slums. Education, too, disappeared. As did any medical care.

Into this world, Mok was born.

PROLOGUE

OLD NEWYORK—A.D. 2076. A few hours earlier, the old man had stepped into Old Newyork off the ferry from Mainside. Then it had been dark, with only scattered fires glowing in the night. Now, with dawn fully upon the slums, hazy sunlight gave thin shadows to weeds that sprouted in the cracks of buckled street pavement. Many of the abandoned buildings were black from long-past fires. And ahead, ancient skyscrapers filled the skyline. Their shattered windows showed broken-tooth gaps across their concrete faces.

Few people walked the streets yet. Those who did either darted quick hungry glances in all directions or kept their heads down. The choice was simple in Old Newyork. Hunt—or be hunted.

Rotting garbage made the air sour. Occasional distant screams echoed through the street canyons, haunting the otherwise grim silence.

It filled the old man with sadness. He had expected decay since his last sight of Old Newyork many years earlier, but nothing this bad.

To return to Old Newyork, the old man had given up his name, his wealth, and his freedom. Less than twenty-four hours earlier—before he had stepped onto the steel ferry—he had been the single largest shareholder of Benjamin Rufus Holdings. The giant Internet corporation had assets in the billions.

Mainside, his name—Benjamin Rufus—commanded respect and sometimes fear. It would mean nothing here in Old Newyork. Welfaros did not read newspapers or get daily newsclips on multivid screens.

Mainside, his income was so great he could not hope to spend in a year the interest it earned in a single day. Here, where computer I.D. credit chips were worthless, the only currency he could carry was cash. He could not reach any of his wealth through bank machines or electronic transfers. In days or a week or a month, he would be as poor as any Welfaro. And have as little hope.

Most costly of all was the freedom that Benjamin Rufus had given up by leaving his Mainside mansion and crossing the Hudson River.

Criminals were sent to Old Newyork instead of prison. And only rebels and outcasts actually chose to take the ferry into Old Newyork. In Old Newyork, there were no hospitals, no police, and no electrical power. In the slums, warlords and gangs reigned supreme.

Benjamin Rufus knew that his ride on the ferry had been a one-way trip. Because Old Newyork was a prison, the World United government did not allow anyone to return Mainside for any reason.

And escape was impossible. Three rivers trapped Old Newyork in a triangle. The Mainside shores of all three rivers were dotted with explosive mines. Beyond the mines were high electric fences, and behind those deadly fences, soldiers endlessly patrolled with guard dogs. Patrol boats waited for anyone who tried to swim, drift, or boat to freedom.

As Benjamin Rufus walked and gazed at the horror of the slums, he fought despair. Dwelling on hopelessness would serve no purpose. He had much to do in the next days. So he squared his shoulders, forcing himself to pretend strength with every painful step.

Shuffling shoe leather alerted Rufus to people behind him. He moved to the side of the street to let them pass. It was a family—father, mother, boy, and girl—all in ragged dark clothing. They huddled together in fright as they walked slowly toward the center of the slums.

"Where will we stay tonight?" Rufus heard the boy ask. "What will we eat?"

The family moved on before he heard the father's reply.

Benjamin Rufus pulled his long coat tighter around himself. He decided to follow them. He knew too well about the work gangs in Old Newyork. If this family had just stepped off the ferry, they, too, would soon find out how . . .

Even before Rufus finished his thought, three men stepped into the street, blocking the family's progress. The lead man—with dark greasy hair to his shoulders—carried a loaded crossbow. He pointed it at the father's chest. The other two—both shaved bald—carried spears made of knives strapped to short poles. All three wore black leather jackets and black leather pants.

"Far enough," the lead man grunted. He caught sight of Benjamin close behind the family. "You, old man, join this pitiful group."

Rufus stepped forward. The girl began to cry quietly. Her father put his arm around her. One of the bald men jabbed the father with his spear and forced him to move his arm.

"You'll be coming with us," the leader laughed. "We need you to work as slaves in our factories."

"Slaves? Factories?" The father's voice was strained. "We did not come here to work as slaves."

The leader raised his crossbow to the father's head. "Slaves. You'll wear our tattoos and be our slaves."

Benjamin Rufus stepped through the small family and stood in front of the father. The leader pointed the crossbow at Benjamin's neck.

"Explain," Rufus said, showing no fear. "Tattoos?"

The leader laughed. Breath as horrid as sewer waste blew across Benjamin's face. "You newbies are so dumb. You're always surprised to learn that most people become slaves here. Like Old Newyork is actually going to be better than Mainside for people without money."

He turned his head to show a tattoo on his cheek. It was a crudely drawn scorpion. "See this? We mark you to make you one of ours. Stay in our territory, and you're safe. You get foodstamps as long as you keep working for us. We keep you safe from gangs in other territories."

"No," the father said. "We're here to get away from government control. We came here to live our own lives. We'll make our own way."

The leader snorted. "That was your dream? Well it just ended. Here's how it is in Old Newyork. Five gangs. Five territories. We found you first, you take our tattoo. Not many people make it without tattoos."

It had been years since Benjamin Rufus had needed to respond to a physical threat. But here, in Old Newyork, he was a world away from conference rooms and business deals. Here, in Old Newyork, he had to depend on the reactions of his old, illness-weakened body.

Rufus uttered a silent prayer and pressed his right elbow against his side. It released a 'tric shooter from a strap attached to his forearm, hidden beneath the sleeve of his coat. The shooter slid down into his hand.

With a calm smile, Rufus lifted his arm and pulled the trigger.

An arc of blue light crossed between him and the leader. It hit the leader in the chest and froze him. Rufus snapped off two more quick shots, volting the spear man on the left and then the one on the right. All three stood rigid for a few more seconds, then fell.

"'Tric shooter!" the boy said, his voice filled with awe.

Rufus looked up and down the street to see if anyone else had noticed. It appeared safe.

Rufus stooped and went through the pockets of the fallen men. He stood up holding folded sheets of foodstamps. Rufus gave them all to the wide-eyed father.

"Take this," Rufus told him, "and the crossbow and spears. With the stamps and weapons and God's grace, you'll find a way to support yourselves before you get desperate enough for the factories."

He accepted their thanks and strode as quickly as he could toward the skyscraper street canyons. He did not have much time. His shooter would only be effective as long as it held its electrical charge. He couldn't fight these human wolves forever.

As he walked, Benjamin Rufus noticed the despair had been lifted from him. Helping this family had given faces to his goal. The children and the poor of Old Newyork were why he'd left Mainside, abandoning his name, money, and freedom.

And these people were why Benjamin had left a secret Committee behind on Mainside to continue his work long after he died in Old Newyork.

CHAPTER 1

MAINSIDE—TWENTY YEARS LATER (A.D. 2096). On the tenth floor of a luxury high-rise on the other side of the river, a group of twelve men stood in a large room. The only other items in the room were a high padded cot, as large as a single bed, on wheels . . . a life support machine . . . and a nitrogen-cooled computer.

On that cot lay Mok's motionless body, draped with a sheet. Two nurses tended to the body. Monitor lines ran from the young man's head to the computer. Other lines from various parts of his body ran to the life-support machine. The steady blip of his heartbeat echoed in the silence of the room.

"Most of you have seen this young man on our vidscreen in the other room," the man named Cambridge said. "I thought you should see him in real time, not virtual reality."

Cambridge was tall and thin, with nearly white hair. Although he wore a cashmere sweater and blue jeans, nothing else about him was casual. His hawklike appearance, the intensity in his eyes, and his reputation set him apart from the other members of the Committee.

"I'm glad we had a chance to see this," one

Committee member said. "It makes him more real for us when we talk about him."

Some of the Committee members wore business suits. Others the latest fashions in training gear even though none actually went to the workout centers. All of them were in their forties and fifties. These were successful, commonsense men who did not need to wear the black silk togas of Technocrats to boost their egos.

"As you can see," Cambridge said to the whole group, "the monitors show Mok is in no physical danger."

"And he has passed the first step," another said. "He was not killed in the prison in Egypt.

"He also refused to kill an innocent man."

"An uneducated Welfaro," a member marveled. "Yet he succeeded where all the others have failed."

"Good thing," another said. "The others, at least, knew they were in cyberspace. They were able to yank themselves out before death struck. This one . . ."

"Yes," a doubting voice added. "This one really believes he is now in a castle. He *has* been cybered to the siege, has he not?"

"Yes," Cambridge said. "He is there, sleeping. You all know how the program works. He is in cyberspace. Around him, the characters and situations have been set up to respond to his decisions. Just as if everything were real."

"And he has a guide?"

"Yes, someone to answer only the necessary

questions. This is a test he must pass without help. He must make his own decisions." For the first time, emotion crossed Cambridge's face. Troubled emotion. "And let us pray he succeeds. You know as well as I do that if he dies in cyberspace, he'll die here too. We have medtechs watching his progress on the vidscreens, but death in the castle could strike so quickly that . . ."

A Committee member interrupted loudly, "Don't pain yourself by bringing up this issue again. His psych-profile showed he would have accepted these risks had we given him the choice. After all, in Old Newyork he faced death at any time. Here, even with those risks, he is far safer. And his future far more promising. As it is, the test will be much more effective if he does not know he is in cyberspace."

Cambridge sighed. "Yes, I do keep telling myself that."

It was obvious Cambridge would never be at ease with the Committee's decision. "Any other comments before we move back to the conference room?"

"No question, but a prediction," the doubter said. "We should prepare ourselves for failure. If the finest of our recruits couldn't pass with all their knowledge and training, this one is doomed for certain."

"Wait before you pass judgment," Cambridge said. A small smile crossed his face. "After we cybered him to the castle siege, he asked about the Galilee Man."

Understanding crossed the faces in front of him.

"Yes," Cambridge said. "Mok is searching through the ages for Christ."

CHAPTER 2

CYBERSPACE—THIRTEENTH CENTURY. *Tap. Tap. Tap. Tap. Tap.*

Mok awoke. He was half sitting, half leaning against one of the turret walls. He was confused by the quiet, persistent tapping sound. The noise worked into his bones. It seemed to come from the very stones of the castle.

Tap. Tap. Tap. Tap. Tap.

"Blake," Mok said, "do you hear that?"

The dwarf did not answer. Mok was not prepared to admit he liked the grumpy little man. Yet Mok knew no one else and had no other place to turn for help.

"Blake? Blake?"

In the land of pharaohs, the little man with a bad temper had appeared from nowhere to offer unrequested advice to Mok. The dwarf had also been beside Mok when he had first arrived at the castle, before Mok had fallen asleep. It figured that the first time Mok truly wanted the dwarf nearby, there would be no answer from him.

Mok stood and opened his eyes wide, straining in the darkness. The dwarf who had been with him earlier had disappeared.

Tap. Tap. Tap. Tap. Tap.

Mok wrapped himself in his coat and settled back

against the wall. Running around in the dark to find Blake would do him little good. There was no sense looking for trouble. Mok closed his eyes and waited for morning.

Tap. Tap. Tap. Tap. Tap.

No need to look for trouble, Mok repeated to himself with bitter humor. He fully believed that dawn would bring it to him.

"Young sir," a voice awakened him, "your father has called for you."

Mok blinked himself into wakefulness. He stood and faced the man. Earlier, Mok would have laughed at the strangeness. This man was dressed in metal armor of dull silver. On his head, he wore what looked like an upside-down bucket with a slit that revealed his eyes. On his feet, he wore iron shoes. Earlier, Mok would have decided it was another dream brought on by impure glo-glo water.

No longer.

Mok's home was the street slums of Old Newyork. It was there that he'd been shot with a blue light by a stranger. It had knocked him unconscious. Mok had awakened in Egypt, a country far beyond his imaginings, centuries earlier.

He had seen a great pyramid and dunes of sand. He'd faced an execution ordered by a pharaoh's daughter. He'd found a way to survive, only to wake up here.

And now he stood on a great castle wall overlooking hills so distant they faded blue against the early dawn. The land outside the castle walls was dark with massed soldiers. And the dwarf—before he'd disappeared—had told Mok these soldiers planned to take the castle and kill everyone inside.

This was far beyond the dreams caused by glo-glo water in Old Newyork. Mok had been thrust into something beyond his understanding. He was finally prepared to admit it. All he could do was watch and wait and hope it might soon come clear.

Because of that, he did not laugh at the man in front of him. Especially since the man carried a great sword on his belt. Instead, Mok waited for the man to speak. During the brief silence they shared, Mok heard the noise that had followed him into sleep.

Tap. Tap. Tap. Tap. Tap.

"I speak for every knight in this castle," the man said. "We are grateful for how you encourage us. Day by day, our men have died by arrows fired from below. Yet despite the danger, you run boldly from turret to turret, bringing water skins, passing along news, lifting our spirits. Without doubt, you are truly noble. No one could deny you are Count Reynald's son."

Count Reynald? Mok wondered. *And "night"? This man calls himself a "night"? Are there those who call themselves a "day"?* Mok reminded himself of his decision to watch and wait. He held his tongue.

The man's sun-blackened face was grim with concern. He seemed a man of great physical power, yet he slumped with worry. This was no moment for Mok to interrupt.

"The castle shall fall soon," the man said. "Leave us here and join your father as he has requested. If you outlive us—as I hope you shall—honor us by remembering how bravely we fought."

Tap. Tap. Tap. Tap. Tap.

"This tapping . . ." Mok said. He cocked his head as if listening to the castle walls.

"Yes, m'lord. It bothers me too. As if you or I need reminder of pickax against stone. The miners beneath the great castle walls chip at the foundations like a toothache gnaws at our skulls. I almost welcome the final fight when the castle walls will tumble, if it will stop the sound."

The knight pointed at a stone stairway. "Your father waits in the inner courtyard. Please inform him we are prepared to fight to the end. We will not go gently."

Mok nodded, trying to understand everything he had heard. His father? A count? From these words, could Mok assume the count ruled the castle?

Mok accepted the man's handshake and walked away in silence. At the stairway, he glanced again over the castle walls at the activity below. Deep ditches had been filled with rubble and broken stones. Hundreds of men pushed great wooden machines over the filled ditches and advanced toward the castle. Thousands of soldiers stood behind them in motionless columns, their distant lances tiny upright lines of black.

Tap. Tap. Tap. Tap. Tap.

And below, miners dug at the stones that supported the castle's walls.

Mok took a deep breath and descended the stone stairway.

CHAPTER 3

AFTER HIS LONG DESCENT to the bottom of the stairs, Mok saw two groups of men ahead in the courtyard. One group stood with horses behind them. Some twenty steps away, the smaller group waited. These men were dressed in the armor of knights. One of the knights motioned for Mok to draw closer.

Mok did so. This was much more than a dream. He had accepted that he could not escape from this strange world. And with no escape, he must live by his wits. It was the only possession he'd carried here from the world of Old Newyork. Mok would listen and try to survive. If they believed he was the count's son, he would act in that manner.

"My son," the man said gently as Mok approached. This, then, was Count Reynald. He placed his hands on Mok's shoulders.

Mok looked at the man with cropped, dark hair and a tired face. He wore a purple cloak. There was a long sword belted to his side.

Count Reynald took his hands off Mok's shoulders and nodded in the direction of the other group. At the front was a short man, red-faced and bald. He, too, wore a fine robe. His fingers were heavy with gold rings. The sword in his sheath was short and curved.

"This is Tabarie, the sultan's messenger," Count Reynald explained. "A brief truce was arranged. He is here under a safe conduct, which I issued. He shall inform us of the sultan's terms of surrender."

"Not until your wife joins us," Tabarie said in a high-pitched voice. "Your entire family should hear this message."

The count pointed at two approaching figures. "She arrives. Along with her servant."

Mok followed Count Reynald's gesture. And nearly fainted. Not at the sight of Count Reynald's wife, a tall woman who walked with dignity. But at the younger woman behind her. The servant was the beautiful Raha—the pharaoh's daughter from the land of Egypt! Here in the castle!

Mok nearly cried out in surprise, but Raha noticed the look on Mok's face. With a grave, gentle shake of her head, she warned against it. Had Mok not been staring at her, he would not have noticed her signal, for no others noticed their brief glance of recognition.

Mok had no chance to wonder about the girl.

Tabarie puffed out his chest and spoke with self-importance. "Listen to me carefully. For your lives are in my hands."

CHAPTER 4

TABARIE PAUSED FOR EFFECT. The sun was hot on Mok's shoulders. When his lungs began to hurt, he realized he was holding his breath.

"No," Count Reynald broke the silence. "Our lives are not in your hands. Nor in those of the sultan who commands you. Our lives are in God's hands."

"Bah," Tabarie spit. "Because of that stubborn belief, you face death instead of freedom."

Tabarie raised his right hand. With chubby fingers, he pointed behind him. "Outside waits one of the greatest armies of all time."

He spit again. "This castle was thought to be a stronghold that no one could conquer. Yet, it took us less than a week to destroy your outer walls. Your moats? Hah! Filled with the rubble of your outer walls. We are already using your castle against you."

Tabarie paused for breath. He was so fat that just the effort of speaking made him wheeze. "And how long did it take us to kill most of your soldiers? Even though you had boiling oil and arrows raining down on us. Although twenty of our soldiers died for every one of yours, in the end, your efforts were useless against us."

Tabarie sneered. "Your peasants—except for this

foolishly loyal servant girl—have deserted you. All that remain are your inner walls, protecting you and a small miserable group of knights. You are running out of food and water. Could it be worse? Hardly. And below, our miners dig at the—"

"We know our situation," Count Reynald said. "I doubt your sultan sent you here to boast."

Tabarie's eyes turned to dark coals. "No, he sent me here to give you his terms of surrender. Give up your castle and faith. In return, you will receive safe conduct to the harbor. Ships can take you, your family, and your knights to England."

"Why do you want surrender?" Count Reynald asked. "You already claim certain victory despite anything we do."

"Two reasons. When the foundation of this castle gives way and the walls fall in, we will destroy you. But it will take time and many lives. The sultan would prefer to save both."

"And the other reason?"

"You and your family will set an example," Tabarie replied. "Give up your castle. Denounce your faith. The people must know that the Christians can no longer claim this land as their Holy Land."

"This *is* the Holy Land," Count Reynald said. "Even if we deny it, the truth will remain. Christ himself walked these lands. He died on a cross in Jerusalem and rose again. That truth will ring throughout the centuries, regardless of how many small and petty men try to deafen its glorious sound."

Mok felt his heart leap. He had spent hours of

his childhood listening again and again to an audiobook that spoke of a man named Christ, the man of Galilee.

Blake, the dwarf now long gone, had spoken of the man of Galilee. And now the name of Christ again! Others *did* know of him!

Was the man legend? Or real? Mok wanted to step between the men and blurt out his questions. He held himself back and vowed he would approach Count Reynald with these questions later. If later they were still alive.

"You will not publicly deny the man called Christ?" Tabarie asked Count Reynald.

"No," Count Reynald replied.

"Then you will die a horrible death."

Count Reynald smiled. Peace shone from his face. "No matter how horrible the death, it will only be fleeting in the face of eternity. We will all pass through the curtain of death to be welcomed home by him."

Tabarie looked at Rachel. "And you servant girl, are you thus prepared? You may still turn your back on these people."

"Because of my loyalty, they treat me as their daughter," she said. "I will stay with them to the end. Nor am I afraid of death."

Mok listened with intensity. Count Reynald was repeating much of what Mok had heard in the audiobook. Yet how could it be? Living beyond death? A home with the Galilee Man? How could a person believe this with such strength that death held no fear?

Tabarie spoke again. "I will give the sultan your foolish answer."

Tabarie turned his back on Count Reynald. The fat man tried to mount his horse. After several clumsy attempts to lift his heavy body, he snapped his fingers. Two of his soldiers helped him into the saddle.

As Tabarie took the reins of his horse, he gave a final backward glance.

"Everything is ready for our final attack," Tabarie said. "In less than two days the sultan's army will be inside this castle. Not one of you will walk out of here alive."

Tabarie settled his cloak over his shoulders. He rode out. After his departure, the clatter of horses' hooves continued to echo in the courtyard.

CHAPTER 5

MAINSIDE—A.D. 2096. One of the Committee members waited for the first chance to disappear safely from the conference room. As he had done earlier, he found an empty stairwell in the building. Again, he pulled a satellite-phone from his suit pocket. He flipped it open to the tiny vidscreen, dialed a number, and waited for the screen to come to life.

It took five rings for His Worldship to answer his private line. The vidscreen in front of the Committee member remained dark—the president had only answered on audio, choosing to leave the visual button alone.

"What is it?" His Worldship spoke with irritation.

The Committee member's own face, then, showed on the vidscreen on His Worldship's end. "This is when you scheduled me to call, your Worldship. On a scrambled signal of course."

"Wipe that smug look off your face," His Worldship said. "Give me the latest report and then get off this line."

While it was considered rude to take incoming video without returning video during a call, the president of the World United could do what he wanted. He was the most powerful person among the billions who had survived the Water Wars.

"As you know, the candidate is fully awake in a Holy Land castle, your Worldship. And the castle is about to fall. Everyone inside will die. I doubt the candidate will find a way to survive. So Cambridge loses both ways. If he leaves the candidate in cyberspace, the candidate is dead. If Cambridge brings him back to real time, the test is over. Either way, the final candidate is finished. And you will win. "

"Let me remind you he did not die in Egypt as you promised he would."

"I am far from worried, your Worldship. There are many ways for the candidate to die."

"Tell me."

"It takes millions of gigabytes to construct a cyberspace world real enough for the subject to believe he exists within it. Because of that, there are boundaries."

"Boundaries?"

"Think of it as a movie set, your Worldship. The Welfaro is in a thirteenth-century castle. He sees the people within the castle walls and the army beyond. But a program this complex strains the available memory on the super computer. Only enough cyberspace setting is built to make it believable. Beyond the castle walls, there is a cybervacuum. In this program, if Mok actually leaves the castle, he will step into that cybervacuum. The shock will short-circuit his brain."

"In other words," His Worldship said, his voice less harsh and more satisfied, "if he stays in the castle, he will be killed. If he survives and flees the castle, he will die."

"Yes, your Worldship."

"Good."

His Worldship hung up on the Committee member.

In the stairwell, the man took several minutes to compose himself before returning to the Committee.

CHAPTER 6

CYBERSPACE—THE THIRTEENTH CENTURY. After the sultan's messenger left, Count Reynald barked out orders for his knights to guard against an attack. In the confusion, Mok was left to wander.

He followed the count's wife and her servant, determined to wait until the servant girl was by herself. If she truly was Raha, the pharaoh's daughter, she could explain to Mok how they both had gotten here from ancient Egypt.

For twenty minutes, Mok did not get the chance to question her. He followed at a slow pace, always staying just out of sight of the two women.

And always, he heard the quiet sound of miners digging at the foundations of the walls, the quiet sound of horror. *Tap. Tap. Tap. Tap. Tap.*

Mok tried not to think what the sound meant. He tried not to think of the sultan's threat and the army beyond the walls. *Tap. Tap. Tap. Tap. Tap.*

Mok found it easier to ignore the sound when he put his mind on the servant girl. How had she followed him through time? Did she know how he had been taken from Old Newyork? And, more important, did she know why?

As the two women walked along the castle's

inner walls, they stopped to encourage knights and soldiers at their various posts. During their wide-ranging stroll, Mok began to understand the defense system of the castle.

The outer walls—which the army had torn down to fill the ditches—were only the first defense. Between the outer walls and the inner walls were some of the town buildings, long since burned to the ground. The inner walls had not fallen yet and formed a large square. It was on one of these walls that Mok had first found himself in this land.

Inside the walls was the large courtyard where Mok had listened to the terms of surrender and had first seen Raha. Placed around the courtyard were different buildings—stables, a carpentry shop, a blacksmith, an oven room where bread was baked, a kitchen, and a place for the soldiers to sleep.

Finally, at the far end of the courtyard was a tall round tower made of stone. Mok compared it to some of the buildings in Old Newyork and decided it was at least four stories tall. It was protected by sharpened poles sticking outward from its base. There was only one entrance into the tower—halfway up the solid face of stone. A set of narrow wood stairs led to that door.

It was not difficult for Mok to figure out the purpose of the building. It was the final defense. A place for all to retreat to when the inner walls fell.

It also became the place where Mok could finally speak to the servant girl. As the count's wife and the girl neared the huge tower, Mok stayed well behind and out of sight. The count's wife continued on toward the stables. The servant girl began to climb the narrow stairs leading to the tower's entrance. As the count's wife stepped into the stables, Mok ran across the open space to the stairs.

He dashed up them. The servant girl waited for him at the top. Her hand was on the key she had just inserted into the lock of the door.

Mok stopped two steps short of the top and looked up at her.

"Yes?" she said. Her frown showed she found Mok's activity unusual.

"I need to speak to you," he said.

It was her. He knew it. The same slim height. The same shoulder-length black hair. Only now she wore not a luxurious linen wrap but a plain blue dress. Gone was the gold band that had circled her forehead. Gone also was the jewelry and perfume.

"If you want to speak with me, all you need do is command," she said. "You are the count's son."

Mok's chest heaved as he sucked in a breath and pondered what he might say next.

"Then go on inside," he said when his breath returned. "For I have many questions."

"Will you allow me to continue my task as ordered by my lady?"

Mok nodded agreement. The door creaked on leather hinges as she let them both inside.

Without speaking, she entered the shadowed coolness of the tower. Mok followed and said nothing at first. He was too busy looking around as they wound through corridors and climbed more steps. He could see because shafts of sunlight came through square windows cut in the rock. Carpets hung from the walls, decorated with scenes of hunters chasing deer through forests. Open doors to some rooms showed bed chambers, with lavish rugs on stone floors. They passed a small kitchen, an oven, and a weapons supply room.

Mok was glad that the hallways and rooms were empty of other people. He wanted as much time as possible alone with this servant girl.

She climbed a final set of stairs and stepped out through a small door.

He crouched to get through, then almost gasped when he straightened in the dazzling sunlight. They were on an open walk at the top of the tower, with waist-high walls around the edges.

"What business do you have here?" he asked.

She pointed at a small cage resting on a ledge. It was filled with pigeons.

"I have a message to send," she said, holding out a small strip of white. "Would you like to read it before I tie it to the pigeon's leg?"

Mok could not read. No one in Old Newyork ever learned. But he was not about to tell her that.

"Where will the pigeon go?" Much as Mok wanted to demand other answers, this matter interested him.

She gave him another frown, as if he had asked a stupid question. "Where it was born. A town along the sea, some forty miles to the north. Our message is sent to let them know we have not given up."

"That is one of the matters I want to discuss," Mok said, "why we do not surrender. But first, the other matter . . ."

He stepped forward and grabbed her wrists. "Tell me what is going on here. I know you are the pharaoh's daughter!"

Without warning, she stamped her heel down on his toes, crushing the small bones in his foot. Mok hopped backward in pain. He lost his balance, spun around, and fell. The low wall caught him squarely in the stomach.

For a second, he teetered over the wall. Far, far down were the sharpened poles.

She grabbed his hair and yanked him back.

He stood tall, panted, and stared at her.

"You'll get no apology from me," she said. "You may be the count's son, but you have no right to do what you did."

"And you have no right to keep up this mystery," Mok said, angrily. "Tell me what game you play."

"The sun has baked your head," she told him. "I play no game."

"You are Raha. A pharaoh's daughter. You tried to execute me."

She laughed. "My name is Rachel. I'm a servant girl. And you are a fool."

Mok glared at her. At that moment, he truly doubted his own sanity. Before he could say another word, however, a whistling scream drew his attention. It ended in a giant roar. And the tower shook beneath them.

CHAPTER 7

MOK ROCKED BACK AND FORTH on his feet. It felt like the entire stone tower had wobbled.

"What was that?" he asked.

Rachel pushed her hair back from her face. She calmly opened the cage, stuck in her hand, and pulled out a pigeon. She tied the message to the bird's leg.

"I expect that was the beginning of the new attack," she said. With a gentle throw, she tossed the pigeon into the air. It circled once on whirring wings, then cut a straight line across the sky.

There had been a time when Mok believed the events around him to be a wild dream. He had enjoyed the experience then, hoping he might never wake. Now, in confusion and fear, he wished desperately to open his eyes and find himself in his sleep tunnel beneath Old Newyork.

"But what was it? I mean—"

Before he could finish his question, another whistling scream grew louder. A movement caught the corner of his eye. Then seconds later, the roar. Followed by another tremor of the tower.

"A rock," he said with awe. "A rock the size of . . ."

"A chariot," Rachel said. There was no emotion

in her voice. "Fired from a catapult. They are close enough now to hit this tower."

"Anything else?" Mok asked sarcastically, thinking nothing could be worse.

"Oh, they have a rope-wound bow. It takes three men to crank. The giant arrow is released with such force that it will go right through a wooden door. Or a man. And when they get closer, they have giant battering rams. With dozens of men behind them, they can run through a wall. And, of course, the burning buckets of pitch shot from smaller catapults."

She put her hands on her hips. "But why, my young lord, do you pretend to know none of this? You saw it all as they tore away the outer walls."

She was truly not Raha? She was simply as she said, a servant girl, who fully believed Mok was the son of Count Reynald?

Mok closed his eyes. He wanted to weep in frustration. So many questions. And not even one answer.

Another shrieking whistle. Followed by the explosion and shuddering walls.

"Please," Mok said, "help me."

"My lord? You do not look well."

"Pretend I am a stranger, just dropped inside these castle walls," Mok said. "Explain why the army has attacked. And why Count Reynald would follow the man named Christ into death."

Rachel studied him to see if he were joking.

Mok's face must have showed the anguish and confusion he felt. Her frown relented and her own face softened.

26

"Sit beside me," she said. "Unless a rock lands right on top of us, we will be safe here. These walls should stand for at least a week."

She sat and drew her knees up. "Why has this army attacked? A few hundred years ago, great Crusades were fought to conquer this land. Now, we in turn are being conquered. By Mamelukes. Long ago, they were slaves brought to serve the Turks of this region. They revolted against the Turks, and have begun to lay claim to the entire Holy Land. Our castle is the last stronghold of Christian knights remaining."

"The Holy Land . . ." Mok whispered. "Tell me about the man from Galilee." Even with the rocks thudding into the walls, Mok had to know. From his childhood, he'd wondered about this man. And here, finally, was someone who might know.

"The man from Galilee," she repeated softly. "He was born nearly 1300 years ago. This is the year 1296, and history is marked by his birth."

"He was that important," Mok mused. The sunlight warmed his shoulders. All he could see was the line of the low walls and the blue sky beyond. If it weren't for the catapulted rocks, it would have been a peaceful place to talk to a beautiful girl. "This man from Galilee must have been a king. An emperor. Or even more important."

"He was a simple carpenter," she said, smiling. "A man who made his living by working wood."

"Only a carpenter? But how—"

Her smile broadened. As teacher, she was enjoying

the response of her student as she guided him in his understanding of the Galilee Man.

"He was alive on this earth for only thirty-three years. Yet because of him, we are here in the castle thirteen centuries later. Over the last two hundred years, our armies have fought to protect the Holy Land for pilgrims who wish to visit the land of his birth."

"How could one man have such impact?" Mok asked.

"Because," she said. "He is the Son of God."

"*Is?*" Mok asked. "Not *was?*"

She opened her mouth to reply but stopped as a trumpet blare echoed in long, mournful blasts.

She stood quickly and pulled Mok to his feet.

"That is a signal calling every person to the walls," she said. "We must join them in the battle!"

CHAPTER 8

MOK STOOD ON TOP of the thick stone walls that formed the final protection to the courtyard. He could hardly believe his eyes. Below him, swarms of soldiers advanced in waves.

A few steps away on each side of Mok were knights in full armor. They formed a line up and down all the walls. Mok had counted earlier. Fewer than two hundred men.

And below?

Thousands upon thousands of soldiers.

What frightened Mok the most was their silence. They moved ahead almost grimly. No war cries to give them false courage, just quiet determination to finish their task.

Behind those soldiers were their great war machines. Creaking on wooden wheels were huge catapults. Behind the catapults, men pushed the long battering rams.

The soldiers moved easily over the filled moats.

The knights atop the castle walls were also silent as they waited for the soldiers to near the castle.

Then the first wave of soldiers reached the walls. They began to throw grappling hooks upward. These were like huge fishing hooks, attached to thick rope. The iron hooks clanged over the stone walls and held. Soldiers grabbed the ropes and began to climb.

Still the knights did not move.

Count Reynald waited until the soldiers below had almost reached the top.

"Now!" Count Reynald shouted.

His knights slashed downward with their swords, cutting the ropes. The climbing soldiers fell backward onto soldiers below them.

At the same time, other knights rolled head-sized boulders over the walls. The bottom of the thick walls curved outward. The boulders followed the curve at high speed, bouncing into the ranks of soldiers below.

Yet other knights began firing arrows. And the women who remained in the castle poured buckets of heated oil over the walls.

The sultan's army did not slow the attack.

For every fallen soldier, three others replaced him. More grappling hooks reached the stone walls. More soldiers below fired arrows upward.

And so the grim battle continued for hours.

Whenever Mok could, he looked around. He did not see one fallen knight. Such was the advantage of a position on top of the stone walls.

But how long could their supply of rocks and arrows and oil hold? How long could they continue to cut ropes before exhaustion set in? Even now, Mok was so thirsty he could hardly move. Only desperation kept him fighting.

If the enemy soldiers managed to crest the walls . . .

One hour of fighting. Two. Then three.

Suddenly, it ended. Just as everything looked lost, just as the knights were falling from fatigue, the army below began an orderly retreat.

Mok did not have to wonder long at the reason.

From far away, he saw the single line of horses riding toward the castle. At the lead was Tabarie, the messenger from the sultan. He carried a long pole with a white flag waving at the top.

None of the knights fired arrows at him or the other riders.

At the castle doors, he reined his horse to a stop.

"Open your doors!" Tabarie shouted up. "The sultan has another message!"

"Move your army farther away," Count Reynald shouted down in a ragged voice. He did not want them to pour in through the open doors, not after all the effort to keep them from swarming over the top of the walls.

Tabarie ordered his army back and waited on his horse. Finally, Count Reynald judged it was safe to open the doors.

Mok joined Count Reynald and his wife and Rachel in the courtyard to listen to Tabarie.

THE CASTLE COURTYARD. *Tap. Tap. Tap. Tap. Tap.* The miners below continued their work, blind to the events above.

In the courtyard, Tabarie's face was shiny with sweat. It took two servants to help him off his horse. He dusted off his cloak with deliberate slowness, knowing that Count Reynald and the others had no choice but to wait.

"A valiant fight," Tabarie finally said. His efforts at dignity were lost when he wiped sweat from his face with a small cloth. "The sultan is impressed at your braveness. He would rather not destroy such good men. That is why he called back his soldiers."

"We will not surrender," Count Reynald said, "unless the terms have changed."

Tabarie did not answer. Instead, he snapped his fingers. Sweat had made them greasy, and no noise resulted. With a look of irritation, he turned his head and shouted at his servants.

They began to move as if according to a plan.

One of the servants unrolled a measuring line. Another took the end of the line and trotted away from the inner courtyard toward the castle gates.

After five minutes of positioning and repositioning the line, and after much rapid discussion in a language Mok could not understand, the two servants nodded agreement at their measurements. A third servant produced a piece of chalk and stooped to draw on the round, flat stones of the courtyard floor.

The sun had begun to settle, and long shadows filled the courtyard.

Except for the scratching of chalk and the eerie *tap, tap, tap* that never ceased, it was silent as the servant drew a circle almost half the size of the courtyard. The servant straightened and nodded that his task was complete.

Tabarie spoke again. "Not only have we undermined your outer walls, but we have also dug beneath your inner courts. Below this circle lies the cave our slaves have mined over the last six weeks. By noon tomorrow, it will finally be complete."

Count Reynald looked at the circle. "As you say."

Tabarie smiled. "The cave is propped with wooden beams. We will pile brush inside. Unless you surrender by tomorrow evening, we will light the brush. Once we start the fire below, the courtyard floor and the walls around it will crack in the heat and collapse. Your great tower will topple. And the sultan promises that his soldiers will not leave a single person inside alive."

"Your terms of surrender?" Count Reynald said. "The same as before? If so, we refuse. Our souls are more important to us than our lives."

"The terms have changed," Tabarie said. "Indeed, you will not be asked to deny the Christ Jesus you call Savior."

"Then we accept."

"Not so fast." Tabarie smiled. "*You* need not deny the Christ. Yet the sultan says he still needs a public denial from this family. The sultan has said it will satisfy him if it comes from your son."

Tabarie turned to Mok.

"What do you say?" he asked Mok with a sly grin. "Will you denounce the Christ? Will you tell the people of this land that you do not believe in him or his cause?"

CHAPTER 10

ALL EYES IN THE COURTYARD turned upon Mok. He swallowed, trying to get moisture into his suddenly dry mouth.

"Your father has made a declaration of his beliefs," Tabarie said. "You need not die for his stubbornness. And a simple word from you will save him. Let me ask again. Does he speak for you? Yes or no."

The seconds moved as slowly as the shadows that crept across the courtyard.

Tap. Tap. Tap. Tap. Tap.

Mok swallowed again.

Tap. Tap. Tap. Tap. Tap.

Below them, slaves widened the cave.

Tabarie stepped closer to Mok. "Think carefully before you answer. I now place not only your life in your hands, but also your father's and your mother's. Indeed, speak up against these foolish beliefs, and you shall save every person still alive within these walls."

"Son . . ." Count Reynald tried.

"Silence," Tabarie snapped. "He has a will of his own. Let him speak for himself. The sultan will take as much satisfaction in the son's denial as in the count's. Across this land, his word will suffice as yours. And we will be freed of the Crusaders and their beliefs."

Tap. Tap. Tap. Tap. Tap.

The pickaxes below sounded much louder in the concentrated silence that fell upon the group. All stared at Mok and waited for his answer.

Mok thought of his audiobook and the man from Galilee. A man who promised a home to lost children.

If the Galilee Man was real—something Mok was determined to discover—would Mok find the home he wanted to believe waited for him? He thought of the lonely fearful nights he had spent in the concrete caves of Old Newyork, wishing his father and mother had not died. He had had only the audiobook and its promises to comfort him.

Yet . . .

Yet what if the Galilee Man were only legend? What if the stories were only stories, meant simply to comfort small children? By speaking against a man who might only be legend, then, Mok could save these people. What could it hurt to denounce a legend?

Mok remembered something from the audiobook. *Don't be afraid of people. They can only kill the body. They cannot kill the soul.*

Mok saw the determination on Count Reynald's face, on his wife's face. These two were willing to die for what they believed. There must be a good reason for it, he told himself.

A carpenter who lived only thirty-three years.

Yet in the centuries that followed his death, armies have fought for him.

Legend or truth?

Could the man of Galilee truly be the Son of God?

In a flash, Mok realized that was the single greatest decision to be made in any life. Legend or Son of God. For if the man of Galilee was the Son of God, every life must be lived in the light of that great truth. A truth that would echo through the centuries.

"Well," Tabarie said, "answer me. Your life depends on it."

"Son," Count Reynald said, "your soul also depends on it. Which is of more importance? A brief life on earth, no matter how painful? Or an eternity of love beyond this life?"

A strange feeling of peace filled Mok. He remembered, too, as a child listening to the audiobook, there had been times it seemed the Galilee Man stood right beside him.

"I stand with Count Reynald," Mok said. "I stand beside him with the man from Galilee."

Tabarie glared at them.

"Tomorrow," Tabarie said, "go to the turrets of your castle. Watch for a long line of slaves carrying brush and wood into the depths of the earth below our feet. And tomorrow evening? Prepare for the fire that will bring the walls down so that our soldiers may massacre you."

CHAPTER 11

MAINSIDE. At his Mainside home, the Committee member sat in his private office. Here, not even his family dared interrupt his work or thoughts.

The office was lined with dark oak wall panels. The desk in it was large, almost empty except for a vidphone. The phone itself was small, but the vidscreen was the size of a television. The Committee member stared at it, biting his nails as he waited.

When the phone rang, he punched the receive button, cutting the ring to silence.

"You answered quickly," the face in the vidscreen said.

"Your Worldship!"

"You were expecting someone else?" the president of the World United asked. The large screen clearly showed the man's sneer. The man's face was stretched tight in the highly fashionable manner of reconstructive surgery.

"I've been paged to expect a conference call with all of the Committee members," he replied, forcing his own face not to show nervousness. As clearly as he could see the president, the president could see him.

"Then my call is timely. Something has happened. Correct?"

"Correct, your Worldship. The Welfaro candidate

is well into the next cyberstage. He was given the choice of denying Christ or facing death when the castle falls. He chose death."

"This is not a good thing," the president said. He stroked his chin as he spoke.

"There is nothing to fear. If the candidate dies in cyberspace he dies in—"

"You've explained that to me a dozen times. No, you fool, I am disturbed for another reason. Have you no concept of history?"

"Your Worldship?"

"David and Goliath. Joan of Arc. Billy Graham. All it takes is one to turn the tide of history. Something about deep childlike faith arms them against overwhelming odds. I will not underestimate our opponent."

"Is it time to send someone in, your Worldship? We have a sequence code for emergencies. Perhaps an assassin in cyberspace . . ."

"Let me think on that," the president said. "For now, I believe it will serve our purpose if the Committee thinks it is safe from interference. On the other hand—"

An urgent beeping interrupted.

"Your Worldship, the conference call has arrived."

"I am not finished with you."

"Your Worldship, if I do not answer, Cambridge will wonder what was more important than a Committee gathering."

"Fine. I will talk to you later." The president hung up.

The Committee member punched another button on the phone and the vidscreen immediately divided into twelve rectangles. Each was filled with a face, including his own.

"Welcome," Cambridge said. His was the face in the top right of the screen.

All the Committee members greeted each other.

"Let's not waste time," Cambridge said. His voice sounded hollow on the speaker phone. "As you know, Mok has passed this second test. With the help of the Living Spirit, he has made a public profession of his faith, even against the threat of death."

Murmurs filled the speaker phone. The one Committee member who had predicted failure had the grace to bow his head.

"Yet," Cambridge continued, "in private conversations with some of you, a serious matter has been brought up. Some of you believe it is a faith untested, for the walls have not fallen. Some of you say he must actually have a sword to his throat for the threat of death to be real."

The murmurs grew as all began to voice their opinions.

"Enough," Cambridge said. "Time here is also time in cyberspace. We must come to a decision soon. Do we let this cybersegment continue until Mok is at the verge of death? Or do we send him to the next stage immediately?"

The voices grew louder.

"Gentlemen," Cambridge called.

In the new silence, Cambridge spoke quietly.

"There is a third option. This candidate has proven himself to be resourceful. What if he finds a way to escape the siege? You all know that if he moves into a cybervacuum beyond the boundaries of this program his brain will be scrambled."

"Escape is impossible," the doubting Committee member snorted. "You know we built this model on an actual siege in the Holy Lands of the thirteenth century—every detail is the same, right down to the sultan's messenger drawing a chalk line of the cave below. No one escaped then. He will not escape now. I say leave him there until he is tested at sword point."

"If we miscalculate by a single second," Cambridge said, "the sword might take his life. And then our final candidate is gone forever. And with him, all our hope."

"This stage was meant to test our candidate's faith to the utmost," the doubter said. "Why move him to the next stage unless we have done exactly that?"

"It is not my role to answer," Cambridge replied. "Instead, I put it to all of you in a vote."

They voted.

Six to five, they decided to leave Mok in the castle about to fall to thousands of soldiers.

CHAPTER 12

CYBERSPACE. In the castle courtyard, four stood in a circle holding hands—Count Reynald, his wife, Mok, and the servant girl Rachel. Two hours had passed since the sultan's messenger had promised that all would be dead by the next evening.

Tap. Tap. Tap. Tap. Tap.

Night and day, as Mok knew, the tapping below the castle had continued for weeks. Daily it had only stopped—briefly—when one shift of slaves left and another shift replaced them.

Tap. Tap. Tap. Tap. Tap.

Mok knew, too, that past the inner courtyard, past the castle walls, an army of thousands waited to flood the castle, engaging the knights in a screaming, raging battle of spears and swords.

At this moment, however, with the sun just about to set, a soft golden light filled the courtyard with deceptive promise of continued life. The air was still and cool. Except for the echoes of the pickaxes tapping against the stone foundations of the castle, it might have been as peaceful as a cathedral.

The four stood about to pray as if the courtyard truly were a cathedral. Three of them—Count Reynald, the countess, and the servant girl—stood with heads bowed and eyes closed in reverent contemplation. Mok, copying them, stood with bowed head. He was unfamiliar to prayer, however, and did not know it was the custom to close his eyes against distractions.

"Almighty Father," Count Reynald spoke in his low voice. "Our lives are in your hands. When our time arrives, please take us quickly through the curtain of death to the light of your love on the other side."

Mok furrowed his eyebrows. He was beyond wondering how he'd been thrust here from the street canyons and work gangs and rats in Old Newyork. He was beyond believing this was a troubled dream caused by glo-glo pharmaceuds in his water. He was even beyond the perplexing mystery of the girl opposite him, a girl who was playing the part of a servant even as Mok himself had been put into the role of the count's son.

Mok's puzzlement was more basic.

The count prayed to a father. *Was not the man from Galilee called the Son?*

The count also spoke as if this father could actually hear his pleas. *How could this be? And could the man from Galilee also hear whenever one spoke? Could it be this simple?*

Mok nearly spoke his doubts aloud, but the others were so earnest in their prayer that Mok did not dare interrupt.

The Count and his wife began to sing softly, a majestic tune Mok did not recognize. Mok remained silent, staring at the stonework of the courtyard.

Tap. Tap. Tap. Tap. Tap.

Not even the hymn could hide the sound of pick-axes digging closer to their death.

Still staring downward, Mok smiled grimly. He needed no more reminder of his impending death than the markings of chalk just beyond his feet. It was a large circle, showing the size of the hole already dug beneath the castle.

Tap. Tap. Tap. Tap. Tap.

It filled Mok with great sadness to think of these people meekly waiting for the invading horde. Wasn't there something to be done?

Tap. Tap. Tap. Tap. Tap.

Below his feet, slaves patiently kept digging.

Tap. Tap. Tap. Tap. Tap.

How far below? Mok wondered idly. How dark and horrid it must be to work as a slave miner.

Then Mok smiled again. Much less grimly than before. Perhaps Tabarie had given them the answer.

When Count Reynald and his wife finished singing, Mok raised a quiet question.

"Tell me," he said, "in what manner do slaves in this land dress themselves?"

CHAPTER 13

FIVE HOURS LATER—in the middle of the night—they were gathered again in the courtyard. Had there been light of day, the count would no longer have been recognizable as the nobleman ruler of the castle. Gone were his fine robes. Instead, he wore sweat-stained rags. His head was shaved; his face and arms were covered with smudged grease and dirt.

The countess, too, was shaved and equally filthy. Hidden beneath their rags, both wore pouches filled with gold. Mok and the girl matched the count and his wife. Mok's scalp, now stubbled, tingled from the earlier scraping of the razor.

"It was kind of the general's messengers to show us the outline of the cave," Count Reynald murmured. "I pray that what was meant to be a show of force proves to be instead a means of life."

"Shall I go first?" Mok said. "I am ready."

At their feet was a pile of flat stones, pried from the courtyard floor. In the opening in the stone work was a hole just big enough to pass through. The end of a thick rope was coiled near the hole. The other end of the rope was tied to a post at the far end of the courtyard.

"No, my son," Count Reynald replied. "Even

though you devised this escape, I shall go first. There is the possibility I might land among the slaves of the next shift. If so, let me take the fight to them. If it is safe, you must help the women follow me down."

Tap. Tap. Tap. Tap. Tap.

Three knights stood behind them. Count Reynald addressed them with matching softness. "You are certain, my friends, you will not join us?"

"We are certain, m'lord," one answered. "Although the fire will begin tomorrow, the stone may not fall through for hours. And we shall fight hard. Tomorrow night, if the castle still stands and we have a chance to escape in the darkness, we will follow. As for now, we will return to our fellow knights upon the ramparts to help create the diversion. And before dawn, we will cover this hole so the light is not visible below."

"God be with you," Count Reynald said. "May we meet in the seaport as planned."

"And God be with you." The three knights bowed, a motion barely seen in the darkness. They hurried away.

Tap. Tap. Tap. Tap.

Minute followed long minute.

Tap. Tap. Tap. Tap.

Silence. The shift had ended.

"Now," Count Reynald ordered. "We must go now. We have little time."

He did not hesitate. He took the end of the rope and tied it around his waist. He handed a portion of the rope to Mok.

"If it is safe once I have landed below," Count Reynald said, "I will tug twice on the rope."

Count Reynald lowered himself into the hole without further instructions. None were needed. Mok braced himself and played the rope out through his hands. When the weight eased, they waited anxiously. Finally, came two quick tugs on the rope. Mok's rapid heartbeat increased in a surge of added adrenaline.

The plan was working. They would join the slaves below as they filed out of the cave. From there, they would find an opportunity to escape. And to the people of the land, it would be seen as a miracle.

All that was left was to get the countess and the girl safely down the rope. Mok would then follow.

Mok helped the countess lower herself into the hole.

"Thank you," she said. "You found a way for us to leave and still keep our honor and our vows. I know now that we will be safe."

Mok nodded with dignity.

He turned to the girl.

"Please," Mok said, "let me ask one final time. Were you not the pharaoh's daughter in the land of endless sand? Help me understand . . ."

He allowed his voice to trail away, for in the near dark of the courtyard, he could see her move toward him.

"Embrace me," she said. "Tightly."

He had no chance to refuse, for she was in his

arms and pulling him against her. She hugged him, then pulled back.

"Breathe deeply," she commanded.

He was puzzled, but already she was pressing a cloth into his mouth and nose. A sweet, cloying smell seemed to fill the cavern of his brain. He tried to protest. Dizziness, however, sucked the air from his lungs and drove him to his knees.

He felt himself begin to topple. He sank to his knees, then fell, eyes closed.

She must have believed him already unconscious.

"I'm sorry," he heard her whisper, "but this was done to save you."

It was the final sound he heard in the castle.

CHAPTER 14

MAINSIDE. When the computertechs finished reporting all the details of Mok's cybertest, one Committee member inwardly squirmed with disbelief, anger, and fear. Outwardly, of course, he showed the same growing joy expressed by the rest of the Committee.

This Committee member managed to exchange congratulations with a few others before excusing himself from the room on the tenth floor. The entire time his face was a mask, although his thoughts were on a netphone in the main floor lobby of the building.

He had been forced to use it once before in a similar emergency—when Mok had passed the first stage of the test. Then, the Committee member had never dreamed he might have to use it again in the same kind of emergency.

There was one small difference. When Mok had passed the first cyberstage, the Committee member had raced to the netphone. This time, he walked as if his feet were encased in concrete blocks. He was not looking forward to the message he had to send.

It seemed like it took him an hour to reach the lobby and cross the marble floor to the public netphone. He wished the trip had taken twice as long.

Although others were leaving the building through the lobby, the Committee member began to type on the netphone's keyboard. For all they knew, he was checking to see if his family had e-mailed him a message regarding a dinner meeting. If someone came close enough to see otherwise, he would hit the delete key and erase everything from the screen.

The Committee member punched out the private dotcom number of the president of the World United. The system prompted him for his e-mail message. The Committee member's fingers clicked over the keyboard:

> I have just received the report that the candidate is moving into stage three. I had considered this impossible. I fear he will move through this stage easily as it has been designed not to test him, but to teach him. I strongly advise you to give me the go-ahead to send in a cyberkiller. Please respond immediately   time is short.

The Committee member hit the send button and hurried from the lobby.

An hour later, during dinner at a restaurant with his family, he briefly excused himself. There was a netphone on the street corner.

The member punched in his access code to check for new messages. There was one. As expected, it was from the president of the World United.

The member shielded the netphone screen from passersby, and scanned the words.

Candidate must fail. Proceed with cyberk____.

CHAPTER 15

CYBERSPACE—A NEW LOCATION. The strong smell of wine surprised Mok.

"Wake up, you scoundrel!" a loud voice roared.

Hot breath blasted Mok's face with more of the smell of wine. "Wake up! Wake up! The captain will have us for shark bait!"

Eyes still closed, Mok told himself he was prepared for anything. First he had been a royal undertaker for a pharaoh . . . then a count's son in a castle under siege. How could anything surprise him now?

"Wake up! Wake up!" Rough hands shook him.

Mok squinted open one eye and looked into the unshaven face of a man with an eye patch. The wine-stench breath and words came from a mouth of black and broken teeth.

The man jerked Mok into a sitting position. He surveyed Mok and then bellowed with laughter.

"By the depths of Neptune," the man shouted. "Whoever gang-pressed you played a mean, mean joke to shave your head in such a manner!"

"Gang-pressed?" Mok managed weakly. He rubbed his scalp. The stubble was still there from shaving his head at the castle.

"Gang-pressed. You and all the others," the man

shouted in glee. "Fools, the lot of you. It's a simple matter to fill you with wine until we can roll you aboard the ship as crew mates!"

"Crew mates? Ship?" Mok, of course, had not had any wine. He struggled to understand, and became more aware of his surroundings. His bed was a pile of damp blankets in a cramped room of rough wooden beams. It smelled of mold and seawater.

"Ship!" the man shouted. "Of course it's a ship! Weren't you in a harbor town last night? Did you not see the masts and the sails?"

"I did not agree to this," Mok said. He became aware of a rocking motion. The entire room seemed to sway. "Set me free."

More drunken laughter from the man before him.

"But you are free! Free to wander this ship! You can even return to the harbor—if you care to swim among the sharks! Otherwise, welcome to the merriest band of cutthroat pirates to sail the seven seas!"

AUTHOR NOTE

Mok's story is actually two stories. One of the stories, of course, is described in this cyberepisode.

There is also a series story linking together all the CyberQuest books—the reason Mok has been sent into cyberspace. That story starts in Pharaoh's Tomb (#1) and is completed in Galilee Man (#6). No matter where you start reading Mok's story, you can easily go back to any book in the series without feeling like you already know too much about how the series story will end.

This series story takes place about a hundred years in the future. You will see that parts of Mok's world are dark and grim. Yet, in the end, this is a story of hope, the most important hope any of us can have. We, too, live in a world that at times can be dark and grim. During his cyberquest, Mok will see how Jesus Christ and his followers have made a difference over the ages.

Some of you may be reading these books after following Mok's adventures in Breakaway, a Focus on the Family magazine for teen guys. Those magazine episodes were the inspiration for the CyberQuest series, and I would like to thank Michael Ross and Jesse Flores at Breakaway for all the fun we had working together. However, this series contains far more than the original stories—once I really started to explore Mok's world, it became obvious to me that there was too much of the story left to be told. So, if you're joining this adventure because of Breakaway, I think I can still promise you plenty of surprises.

Last, thank you for sharing Mok's world with me. You are the ones who truly bring Mok and his friends and enemies to life.

From your friend,

Sigmund Brouwer

The adventure continues!

Join Mok aboard a ship in

QUEST 3

THE PIRATE'S CROSS

It's a galleon filled with savage pirates.
Mok will bear the symbol of the cross. One man
is going to hunt him down, but there is no
place to run. And behind it all, there remains his
quest for the truth about the Galilee Man.